MOORFIELD
Finds a Friend

'And in a minute more, when he looked around, he stopped again, and said, "Why, what a big place the world is!"

And so it was; for, from the top of the mountain, he could see — what could he not see?'

THE WATER BABIES

MOORFIELD
Finds a Friend

LESLEY YOUNG

Illustrated by JANE COPE

HODDER AND STOUGHTON
LONDON   SYDNEY   AUCKLAND   TORONTO

British Library Cataloguing in Publication Data

Young, Lesley
Moorfield finds a friend.
I. Title   II. Cope, Jane
823.914[J]

ISBN 0-340-53713-2

First published 1990

Published by Hodder and Stoughton Children's Books,
a division of Hodder and Stoughton Ltd,
Mill Road, Dunton Green, Sevenoaks, Kent TN13 2YA

Designed by Peter Sims

Photoset by Central Print & Design, Westerham, Kent
Printed in Great Britain by Cambus Litho, East Kilbride,
and bound by Hunter and Foulis, Edinburgh

The Fight for Sight (Special Appeal)
Royal Patron H.R.H. The Duke of York

Ever since 1805 when the first specialist eye hospital in the world opened in London, Britain has been in the forefront of the fight to prevent and cure eye diseases and blindness. That is what the FIGHT FOR SIGHT (Special Appeal) is all about, prevention of blindness and all the suffering associated with it.

The aim of this major capital fund raising Appeal is to raise sufficient funds to redevelop and enhance the Institute of Ophthalmology on a site which has been acquired immediately alongside Moorfields Eye Hospital.

The Institute is one of the world's leading centres of post graduate research and teaching concerned with the prevention and cure of eye disease and blindness. Moorfields is the world's largest eye hospital. Together they will form the world's finest eye care complex, and the interaction between scientists, surgeons, doctors and patients will offer a real hope of solving many of today's eye problems.

The whole project is costing £52 million, of which some £12.5 million has already been raised from public and private funds. Building work is already forging ahead, and we are determined that this great project to alleviate unnecessary suffering will succeed. A centre of excellence will be created, where the best people in their field can carry out research into the causes and cures of blindness, and where the best young scientists, doctors and surgeons can learn how to cope with the eye problems of the future.

Join us in the FIGHT FOR SIGHT, we need people of vision to help others see the way forward.

Royalties from sales of this book are being donated to the FIGHT FOR SIGHT (Special Appeal).

MOORFIELD

Based on a concept by
James H. Campbell
Chairman and Chief Executive

CAMPBELL & ASSOCIATES

BUCKINGHAM PALACE

As Patron of the Fight for Sight (Special Appeal),
I send you my very best wishes and thanks for your
support of the Appeal by way of this book.

It is vital that we ensure that the world famous
Institute of Ophthalmology can continue its essential
work and research in order that we have the best chance
of winning the fight for the prevention and treatment
of blindness.

'I've booked you a ringside seat,' said Leo's mother. 'Enjoy yourself – and don't talk to strangers.'

'I don't want to go to the circus,' said Leo.

'Go on,' said his mother, 'you deserve a treat – you've spent the first day of your holiday helping me change beds and peel potatoes. You must be bored stiff. Boredom's not good for anyone,' she added, smoothing down her flowered apron.

'Does him good, helping,' mumbled the cook, stubbing out his cigarette too close for comfort to a jelly left to set.

'I've asked you before not to smoke in the kitchen,' said Leo's mother.

Since Leo's father had died, his mother had run a Bed and Breakfast house. Leo did as much as he could to help, which meant that he had little time to make friends. He had heard people at school saying that the famous Roxy Circus had come to town.

Leo shut the door and stepped out into the cold, late afternoon. He took a deep breath and filled his lungs with salty air, getting rid of the smell of cooking fat and lavender polish. At the end of the sea front the Roxy Circus lights were shining. Although it was summer, it was bitterly cold and the sea rose in sharp peaks, like the cream on top of his mother's trifle.

It was too early for the circus to begin, so Leo wandered round the side shows set up near the Big Top. The one he liked best was the Hall of Mirrors. One mirror made him look enormously fat. The next made him look as thin as a pencil. The third mirror made his body look wavy and strange, but his face stared back at him with a curved smile. It looked as if it had a secret. It looked as if it knew something exciting was going to happen.

Leo found the seat with the same number as his ticket and sat down.

The first act was on the trapeze. Leo found after a while that

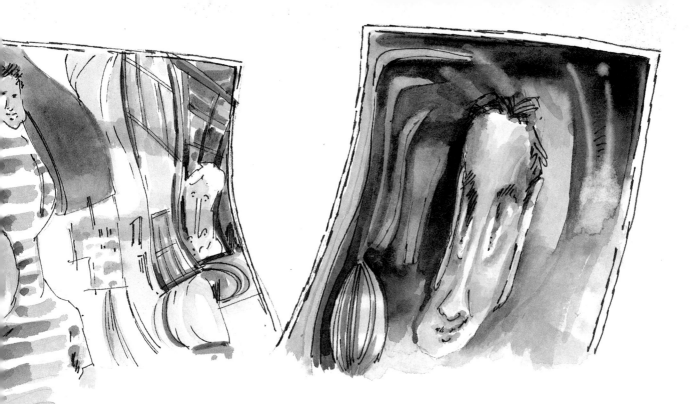

he was getting a crick in his neck, having to look up all the time.

Then the elephants walked solemnly round the ring, each holding the tail of the animal in front. Leo didn't think that there was anything especially clever about that.

The clowns whooped into the ring in an old banger of a car that fell to bits, spilling them onto the sawdust. Lots of people laughed, but Leo didn't think it was very funny. It didn't make him laugh the way his mother did when she was describing the guests in the boarding house.

'You should see the new couple,' she'd say. 'He's wearing his hair back to front!'

Then the ringmaster announced 'An amazing juggling bear'.

Leo leaned forward as a small, brown bear with a long snout padded into the ring.

'A teddy!' said the girl next to him.

The bear juggled jars of honey, catching them in his paws with a soft thud. The ringmaster lit three fiery torches and the bear juggled these, bringing gasps from the crowd.

When he stopped, and held up the torches, the bear looked straight across at Leo. The fire from the torches lit up his eyes, and Leo could see at once that the bear was unhappy. He looked sad and lonely. Leo watched him carefully for the rest of the act, and grew more and more sure that the bear was miserable. He made up his mind to find out why.

When the show ended, Leo set out to look for the bear's cage. At last he found it, tucked away behind the elephant's huge pen. As he got near it, he could hear a deep, sniffing noise.

'Don't talk to strangers,' his mother had said. She hadn't said anything about bears.

The bear looked at Leo with sad, brown eyes. 'Hello?' he said, making it sound like a question.

Leo couldn't tell whether he had a foreign accent or whether all bears spoke like that.

'You are sad, aren't you?' he said, 'Can I help you?'

'This weather,' said the bear, waving a paw, 'this cold wind – it reminds me of my home. I am home-ill.'

'Home-sick,' said Leo. 'Where do you come from?'

'I come from Russia,' said the bear proudly. 'A long time ago, I was playing outside our cave with my twin brother, when the circus people crept up and trapped us in nets.' He shuddered. 'My brother was taken off to one circus, and I was

brought to this one. And since then, I have been travelling all over the world, but I have never seen my twin again.' He sniffed loudly.

'What's your name?' asked Leo.

'Where I come from,' continued the bear, 'is so cold that I always wear a hat with earflaps. So, all I hear – even my name – is,' he paused, 'what is the word – moofled?'

Leo didn't recognise the name. 'Moorfield?' he asked.

'Something like that,' said the bear.

'Well, I will call you Moorfield,' said Leo.

'Thank you,' said Moorfield, 'I don't feel so lonely now that I have a name.'

'And a friend,' said Leo, turning the key on the outside of the cage. 'Look, I've got to get home now, but you must come along later, when all the circus people are asleep.'

He told Moorfield exactly how to find his house. 'You will know it's ours because it's got a B & B sign hanging outside it.'

'This means Boys and Bears?' asked Moorfield.

Later that night, Moorfield swung open the door of his cage and padded between the circus caravans, following his snout to Leo's house. He let himself in and was about to go downstairs to the basement, as Leo had told him, when he stopped. He was very hungry. Excitement always made him hungry, and he realised that he was starving. He would never be able to sleep if he didn't have something to eat.

Moorfield easily found the kitchen by its smell, and looked in the cupboards. There were large, catering-size packs of flour and trays of eggs. He found all the ingredients for his favourite food – pancakes.

Moorfield had watched the circus people cooking often, and pancakes were among their special treats. Like all bears, he had a very strong sense of smell, and he cooked by smell rather than taste.

He found a bowl, spooned in some flour and broke a couple of eggs on top. He mixed in some milk and sniffed the bowl. 'Something's missing. Now, what do they do in the circus at this stage?'

'I know,' he thought, 'they sing a cooking song.'

Moorfield began to stir the mixture in the bowl, and hum softly. As the mixture grew smooth and glossy, he began to sing a Russian folk song. He beat faster and faster and sang louder and louder.

Leo's mother was tossing and turning upstairs, wishing she hadn't finished off the guests' rhubarb crumble. She had dreadful indigestion. Suddenly she heard very strange noises coming from the kitchen.

Creeping downstairs, she looked round the kitchen door and saw a singing bear, his snout deep in her best fruit bowl.

The noise had also woken Leo, some of the guests and the cook. They all gathered in the doorway.

'It doesn't say anything in my contract about bears in the kitchen,' said the cook. 'Anyway, I'm off. I'm fed up with cooking greasy breakfasts.'

'Good!' cried one of the guests, 'We're fed up with eating your greasy breakfasts. And there was cigarette ash on my poached egg this morning. If I may say so,' he added, 'those pancakes smell very good.'

'I just give a final sniff,' said Moorfield, shaking some batter off his snout and getting ready to toss the pancakes. He tossed one in a figure of eight round the light.

'Toss one for me!' said Leo. With a flick of his paw, Moorfield sent a pancake spiralling up to the ceiling, making patterns in the air.

Leo, his mother and the guests sat round the table and feasted on hot pancakes and syrup. Soon they were all feeling warm and full and sleepy.

'This is the best surprise supper I've ever had,' said one of the guests. 'In fact, I want to book for next year.'

'So do we,' cried all the other guests.

Leo took Moorfield down to the basement to make up a bed for him.

In the morning, Moorfield prepared a wonderful spread for breakfast, with another tower of pancakes.

As Leo helped him to clear up, a tear ran down Moorfield's snout. 'You are so good to me,' he sighed, 'But I still miss my brother. How do I find him?'

'Don't worry,' said Leo, 'We'll find him. In fact, we'll start tomorrow.'

The next day, Leo's mother helped him pack a case.

'You deserve a holiday,' she said, 'but if you haven't found Moorfield's brother by the end of the holidays, you must come home.'

Moorfield sat on the case while Leo locked it.

Leo's mother gave him some money in a wallet. 'Take care of that,' she said.

Leo and Moorfield set off towards the port, in the opposite direction from the circus.

'We'll start in France,' said Leo. 'They like circuses in France.'

Leo and Moorfield were walking down towards a ferry, when Moorfield stopped and sniffed the air.

'I smell trouble,' he said.

No sooner had he spoken, than they turned and saw a caravan rounding a corner in the distance. It was towing an empty cage!

'Run!' shouted Leo, 'It's the circus people! I bet the cook told them about you – I never trusted him.'

Moorfield and Leo ran as fast as they could, but just as they reached the ferry, the gangplank went up. The caravan was hurtling nearer and nearer. There was only one thing to do.

'Jump!' shouted Leo, and Moorfield and he jumped into a lifeboat that was tied to the side of the ferry.

The circus people ran from the caravan and rushed to the edge of the quay, but they were too late. The hooter sounded, drowning their angry cries, and the ferry pulled away and set sail for France.

Leo hugged Moorfield, 'We made it. We're on our way.'

As soon as the ferry tied up at Boulogne, Moorfield and Leo jumped off, before the gangplank came down. Then they made their way through the streets, looking for signs of a circus. They stopped at the town square.

'Wait, my friend,' said Moorfield, 'we've had such an exciting day, I'm starving. Can we eat now?' He looked with longing at a table of seafood that stood outside a restaurant. Fat prawns like giant pink commas lay on a platter edged with seaweed. Navy blue cockles shone like spilled ink. A waiter was opening oysters with a small knife and whistling.

'Of course, let's eat,' said Leo, who had suddenly caught the smell of fresh chips coming from the restaurant. 'Do you think they'll take British money?'

But then he stopped and felt through all his pockets again.

'Oh no – my wallet must have fallen out when we jumped into the lifeboat.'

'Don't worry,' said Moorfield. 'Watch me!'

He picked up five oysters. The waiter told him crossly to put them back, but Moorfield was too busy concentrating. The waiter's mouth fell open as Moorfield threw them in the air and began to juggle.

Soon a small crowd had gathered. Then Moorfield took a long strip of seaweed and rolled it into a ball between his paws. He blew on it, opened his paws, and the seaweed had disappeared.

'Bravo!' shouted a large man in a beret.

Moorfield went up to him and pulled the seaweed from behind his ear. 'You've been swimming?' he asked.

Everyone laughed.

When Moorfield stopped, not only had a pile of francs appeared in front of him, but lots of people decided they wanted to eat in the restaurant, just in case he did any more tricks. The owner asked Leo and Moorfield to have dinner on the house, as a thank you. Soon they were tucking into fish and wonderful French chips.

When they had finished their blackcurrant ice cream, Moorfield and Leo set off to find a place to spend the night.

'Thanks to you, we can afford to stay in a hotel tonight,' said Leo to Moorfield.

They came to a huge hotel.

'I'm really tired,' said Leo, 'I think this'll do. It's so big they're bound to have a room.'

'Big?' said Moorfield, 'You should see the hotels we have in Russia!'

Inside, Leo threw himself on one of the beds in their room, and tossed Moorfield a spongebag.

Moorfield shut the door behind him and made sure he could remember what number their room was. Then he padded off down the corridor, looking for the bathroom.

It was all very confusing. He couldn't tell which rooms were bedrooms and which were bathrooms. He was just thinking he would have to retrace his steps, when he saw a pair of mirrored doors at the end of a corridor. They were slightly ajar, and as Moorfield looked at them, he saw himself duplicated lots of times. There were lots of Moorfields, getting smaller as they went back. They reminded him of the Russian dolls that fit inside one another, getting smaller and smaller …

Moorfield was staring at his reflections, when the most amazing thing happened. One of the reflections stepped out of the mirror and raised a paw.

Moorfield's fur stood on end as he realised that he was looking at his long lost twin. He was about to rush forward and embrace him, when a harsh voice rang out: 'Bear!'

Moorfield jumped. But his twin recognised the voice, because he looked very frightened. With a last, pleading look at Moorfield, he turned and ran down the corridor. Moorfield followed him, but he had disappeared.

Dropping the spongebag, Moorfield rushed back to his room. As soon as Leo saw his face, he said, 'What is it?' And then he said, 'You've seen him, haven't you?'

Moorfield sat on the edge of one of the beds. 'I never realised how much I missed him until I saw him,' he said.

'I wish I had a twin,' said Leo. 'Everything is much more fun when there's two of you.'

'Don't worry,' said Moorfield, holding out a paw, 'You've got a friend. And I feel in my fur that our adventures are only just beginning.'